15

JASON WALTRIP '88

ROBOTECH II: THE SENTINELS

Tom Mason & Chris Ulm • *Writers*

Jason Waltrip • *Artist (chapters 1 & 3)*

John Waltrip • *Artist (chapters 2 & 4)*

Clem Robins • *Lettering*

John Waltrip • *Cover Illustration*

Scott Bieser • *Cover Coloring*

Steve Martin • *Back Cover Painting*

Dave Olbrich • *Publisher*

Chris Ulm • *Editor-In-Chief*

Mickie Villa • *Associate Editor*

Dan Danko • *Editorial Assistant*

Tom Mason • *Creative Director*

Material in this volume was previously published in
comic book form by Eternity Comics, a division of
Malibu Graphics, Inc.
Robotech II: The Sentinels #1 (November 1988)
Robotech II: The Sentinels #2 (December 1988)
Robotech II: The Sentinels #3 (January 1989)
Robotech II: The Sentinels #4 (February 1989)

ROBOTECH II
THE SENTINELS ™

VOLUME ONE
MALIBU GRAPHICS, INC.

Other Books Available From Malibu Graphics

Dinosaurs For Hire: Guns 'N Lizards
At last, a sensitive tale of teen-age angst and the trauma of growing up in middle class America. Just kidding! It's really about Dinosaurs with automatic weapons. By Tom Mason. Illustrated by Bryon Carson and Mike Roberts.

The Three Stooges: The Knuckleheads Return
Nyuk! Nyuk! Nyuk! These knuckleheads are back in a collection of seven slapstick adventures! Edited by Tom Mason.

Abbot And Costello: The Classic Comics
Bud Abbot and Lou Costello are reunited in this collection of 20 classic comic stories from their heyday. Edited by Tom Mason.

Spicy Detective Stories
A classic collection of seven two-fisted 1930's pulp detective stories from the pages of Spicy Detective magazine. Edited By Tom Mason.

Ninja High School
An alien princess and a beautiful ninja both want to marry Jeremy Feeple--and they don't care how much of Quagmire High they destroy in the attempt! By Ben Dunn.

Tiger-X: The Adventure Begins
Only one thing can free the United States from Soviet domination--the secret weapon known only as Tiger-X! By Ninja High School creator Ben Dunn.

China Sea
An epic adventure in the tradition of Terry And The Pirates. By Barry Blair.

The Trouble With Girls
Lester Girls would like nothing more than to curl up with a good book in a quiet, suburban bungalow. Instead, he's stuck with a ceaseless round of luscious babes, high adventure, uncountable riches, and break-neck action. By Will Jacobs and Gerard Jones. Illustrated by Tim Hamilton and Dave Garcia.

Scarlet In Gaslight
Sherlock Holmes meets Dracula in the strangest case of his career! By Martin Powell and Seppo Makinen.

Dark Wolf
Priest by day, vengeful killer by night. By R.A. Jones and Butch Burcham.

ROBOTECH II: THE SENTINELS
Graphic Novel
Volume One
Published by Malibu Graphics, Inc.
1355 Lawrence Dr. #212
Newbury Park, CA 91320
805/499-3015
Printed in the USA
First Printing
ISBN# 0-944735-28-2
$19.95/$24.00 in Canada

INTRODUCTION

Chapter I: Beginnings

There we were, sitting on the floor of the Malibu Graphics offices, surrounded by a pile of *Robotech II: The Sentinels* paperwork—scripts, outlines, notes, sketches, diagrams, videotapes, color guides, production breakdowns, memos, character histories—whose sheer bulk resembled the recent Time/ Warner/Paramount takeover.

Unfortunately, most of it—the important stuff, the storyboards, character sketches, and production designs—was in Japanese, and there seemed to be no hope of an accurate translation. To make matters worse, the script for the first issue was due in less than a month. What could two So-Cal beach bums do?

Well, we sat and thought, sat and thought, then thought some more. And slowly, like a giant jigsaw puzzle, the pieces began to fall into place. Here were Rick Hunter (one of the heroes of the First Robotech War), his bride-to-be Lisa Hayes (who didn't do too badly in the war either), Minmei, Jonathan Wolff, General Edwards, Max and Miriya Sterling and their young daughter Dana, Rem and Cabell, Jack Baker and Karen Penn (younger, inexperienced, hot-headed versions of the now-mature Rick and Lisa), the Regent and the Regiss (leaders of the accursed Invid)...and dozens more.

Material was read and re-read. Outlines were drafted. And before long, the script for the first issue came together and was sent to Jason Waltrip for pencilling. In a few short months, the entire issue was completed. Even after completion, one key question remained. *Robotech* fans are an enthusiastic bunch who have taken the characters to their hearts. They were also used to three separate monthly *Robotech* titles from Comico. Would a black-and-white adaptation of never-before-seen material by an all-new company take hold with the fans? We held our collective breaths as the first issue shipped.

Within a week, we had our answer. The mail came in, or more accurately, *poured* in—we were a hit! The first issue sold out in record time and we had to print a second edition within a few short months. And the rest, as they say, is history...

Chapter II: History Lesson

Welcome to the world of *Robotech*. With the scope of Frank Herbert's Dune, the two-fisted action of E.E. "Doc" Smith's *Lensman* series, and the larger than life characters reminiscent of Gene Roddenberry's "Star Trek," the original three *Robotech* animated series—*Macross, Masters,* and *New Generation*—quickly became a phenomenon, sparking a line of toys, games, comics, T-shirts, and a variety of other projects.

But the *Robotech* series, having been created out of several disparate Japanese animated series, left quite a few questions which needed answering. What happened to Rick and Lisa after the final battle with Khyron? How about Minmei? Where did the Invid come from? Did Scott Bernard ever find the SDF-3?

Harmony Gold U.S.A., Inc. and Tatsunoko Studios created *Robotech II: The Sentinels* as a means of tying up these loose ends—filling in the gaps and strengthening the continuity. Plans were finalized to create a series of 65 episodes combining Japanese animation values and American storytelling. (For those unaware of the inner workings of syndicated television, 65 episodes are considered the norm. It allows a series to run 5 times a week—Monday-Friday—for 13 weeks without repeats.) Under the direction of Carl Macek and Ahmed Agrama, new characters were designed, scripts were written, and the first segments were animated. *Robotech II: The Sentinels* was progressing smoothly and set to air in the fall of 1986.

Then everything fell apart. With the devaluation of the dollar against the Yen, the production budget lost 25% of its value overnight. The series was cut back to 36 episodes and finally cancelled.

With one episode finished and another three in various stages of production, the footage from *Robotech II: The Sentinels* was re-edited into a 90-minute movie (now available on videotape from Palladium Books) and the resolution was left to Jack McKinney's five novels. It looked as though *Robotech II: The Sentinels* would never make it into visual form.

Chapter III: Here We Come...

Enter Eternity Comics and its parent company, Malibu Graphics, Inc. We were all fans of the *Robotech* series, and when we heard that the property was available for comic book adaptation, we leapt at the chance. Then the aforementioned mountain of reference material showed up.

As we started to make sense of the material, particularly the interpersonal relationships of the characters, a new problem peered out from beneath the pile: Who are we going to get to write the series? And who has a house big enough to store the reference material? And why is T.R. Edwards referred to as B.D. Edwards in Robotech Art 3?

As editors, we started bouncing ideas off one another, trying to formulate the reference into a cohesive storyline suitable for the cliffhanger style of monthly comics. We outlined the important events—the invasion of Tirol, the refurbished SDF-3, the long-awaited marriage of Rick and Lisa—and developed smaller sub-plots tying up the occasional loose end and giving some of the minor characters a little more screen time. When all was said and done, we had developed more than a story—we had a love affair on our hands. Each of us had our favorite characters and story elements. ("Minmei would never do that!" "Jack should bump into Karen before the wedding!"). Before we knew it, we realized that we couldn't turn the story over to anyone but ourselves. All we needed was the right artist.

Chapter IV: Write Like Demons, Draw Like Crazy!

No one is quite sure where John and Jason Waltrip came from—Jason's samples showed up in our office one day. At the time, we had no work for him. We were still in negotiation for the *Robotech II: The Sentinels* license , and since the final papers hadn't been signed, we couldn't start work yet. We told Jason what we were working on and he mentioned that both he and his brother John were *Robotech* fans. Without prompting, they worked up a number of samples, and when they arrived, we knew we'd found our artists—not one, but two excellent storytellers who were capable of giving *Robotech II: The Sentinels* exactly the look we desired.

John and Jason capture the depth and detail of

the original animated artwork while still retaining a fluid story-telling technique that would translate the action to comics. Alternating issues (Jason does the odd numbered ones, John the evens), they proved excellent technical artists with a firm grasp of composition and design. And, since they were also fierce fans of the original series, they treated the story with the respect of old friends.

Chapter V: The Writing Begins... Or How We Do It

Relying heavily on the original scripts, outlines and the Jack McKinney novels—and throwing in some of our own ideas to flesh out scenes that had been only hinted at—the first issue of *Robotech II: The Sentinels* quickly reached completion. Writing the series, we've reduced it to an almost scientific equation, attacking each script with the ferocity of an Invid invasion.

Once a month—armed with a manageable pile of reference—we get together in one of our favorite restaurants (there's a great place about a minute from the beach) and plot out an issue, breaking it down into a series of short scenes. We make notes, jot down ideas and fragments of ideas, dividing up the scenes that feature our favorite characters (although we occasionally switch characters to give the story a fresh perspective). Once done, the demanding job of actual writing begins.

Every morning, before work, you'll find each of us hunched over his computer poring over the script details and working through problematic sequences. And it doesn't end there. After a hard day's work, one of us will call the other, screaming out a new plot development into the cordless ("Hey! Where's the Regiss during all of this?" "Shouldn't Rick Hunter be in this scene?" "Does Zor have a last name?").

And, like magic, the script is completed three weeks later. Unfortunately, the work is just beginning. John and Jason, depending on the issue number, begin work on the pencilling, sending it to us in three separate installments. Once pencilled, we go back and re-write the script, adjusting the dialogue to fit the pictures, and finding most of the typos. (We do a lot of head-slapping at some of the errors—like misspelling a character's name—which is why we're always grateful for the opportunity to double- and triple-check our work. It's one of the advantages to being your own editor.) From there, the pages go to letterer-extrordinaire Clem Robins, who translates our scripts into balloons and captions and whips up a variety of sound effects with a gazelle-like fervor. After that, it's back to John and Jason for the final inking and the application of gray tones.

Once all of that's done, copies have to go to Harmony Gold U.S.A., Inc. (the *Robotech* owners) for their final approval. (That's standard operating procedure for any licensed project.)

Finally, it's ready to go to the printer for a series of steps whose explanation is about as exciting as watching paint dry. Suffice to say that 30 days later a printed book appears on the newsstands.

One of the things we've tried to do is establish that none of the characters are inherently evil. There are a lot of misunderstandings, hurt feelings, and imagined slights—but every character has a reason for their actions. The Invid desperately need the Flower Of Life—it's the key to their existence. Without it, they die. Would you let anything stand in your way? General Edwards is upset because he's been passed over in favor of Rick Hunter for command of the most important mission in *Robotech* history. Wouldn't that cloud your judgement? And Karen Penn's father doesn't want to lose his daughter to the war machines that killed his wife.

Chapter VI: Where Do We Go From Here?

As this volume goes to press, *Robotech II: The Sentinels* has spawned a companion publication *Robotech II: The Sentinels—The Malcontent Uprisings* chronicling a well-known revolt that took place just prior to the events in *Robotech II: The Sentinels*. It's testimony to the success of *Robotech II: The Sentinels* that a project like *The Malcontent Uprisings* can exist. An original story—not an adaptation of existing material, it's something that no other comic book company has been allowed to do with the *Robotech* characters. The series debuted in August 1989 under the guiding hands of writer Bill Spangler and illustrator Michael Ling.

We've also released *Robotech II: The Sentinels— The Wedding Special*, a two issue limited series chronicling the events of Rick and Lisa's wedding, a limited edition wedding portrait of the entire cast, a full color poster, and this special hardbound graphic novel you hold in your hands, the first in a projected series. Future plans include a new mini-series or two and more than a few surprise appearances by characters you thought you'd never see!

And that brings us to...

Chapter VII: Closing Remarks

By now, our fondness for *Robotech II: The Sentinels* has grown even stronger. Early mathematical geniuses figured out that at our current monthly schedule, the comic will take slightly more than 10 years to complete (10.33 was the exact figure quoted to us). To that we can only reply "So?" Just try prying these characters out of our hands before that.

You now hold in your hands the first four chapters of the *Robotech II: The Sentinels* saga, complete and uncut. What are you waiting for—the moon of Fantoma beckons....

—Chris Ulm & Tom Mason

Special thanks go to Carl Macek, Ahmed Agrama, Jack McKinney, the good people at Harmony Gold (Susan, Lynn and Giselle—take a well-deserved bow) and, of course, all of the fans that have made *Robotech II: The Sentinels* a reality. We couldn't have done it without you!

WHO'S WHO IN ROBOTECH II: THE SENTINELS

A Field Guide To Our Cast Of Characters

Editor's Note: The following is a quick reference guide to the cast of Robotech II: The Sentinels. *Several characters listed do not turn up until issue #2 and #3.*

RICK HUNTER
Commander in Chief of the Robotech Expeditionary Air Force and a hero of the First Robotech War. One of the best pilots, he was trained by Roy Fokker, a casualty of the First Robotech War.

LISA HAYES
Admiral and Captain of the SDF-3. Soon to be the bride of Rick Hunter.

LYNN MINMEI
Celebrity/singer. Lynn Minmei was instrumental in turning the tide of the First Robotech War.

DR. LANG
Leading expert on Robotechnology and civilian leader of the Robotech Expeditionary Force.

MAX STERLING
An outstanding VT pilot, and leader of the REF's famous Skull Squadron. Max is a close friend of Rick Hunter, fighting under him in the first Robotech War. With his marriage to Miriya, Max became the first human to marry a Zentraedi.

MIRIYA STERLING
Originally plotted to assassinate Max during the First Robotech War until they met and fell in love. Her marriage to Max sealed the alliance between the Zentraedi and the human race.

DANA STERLING
The offspring of Max and Miriya, Dana is the first child born of a Zentraedi/human relationship.

VINCE GRANT
The younger brother of Claudia Grant, a hero of the First Robotech War. Vince Grant is also the father of Bowie Grant.

JEAN GRANT
Vince Grant's wife and medical doctor aboard the SDF-3.

BOWIE GRANT
Vince and Jean Grant's son.

GENERAL T.R. EDWARDS
A famous soldier in the civil war before the First Robotech War, General Edwards was the sworn enemy to Roy Fokker, Rick Hunter's close friend during the First Robotech War.

BENSON
General Edwards' assistant and troublemaker.

EXEDORE
Keeper of the Zentraedi history, Exedore was the first of his race to experiment in bio-genetic engineering.

BREETAI
A former Zentraedi Field Commander during the First Robotech War, Breetai's 60-foot frame has been micronized to that of a more normal human—7 feet tall—enabling him to join the Robotech Expeditionary Force.

JONATHAN WOLFF
A Colonel in the Robotech Defense Force, Jonathan Wolff was personally selected by Rick Hunter to lead the infantry forces of the R.E.F.

THE FLOWER OF LIFE
A plant, native to the Invid homeworld of Optera. The fruit of the flower is the only food that gives the Invid strength.

ZOR
A Robotech Master who journeyed to Optera and stole as many of the fruitful plants—The Flower Of Life—as he could, destroying the rest.

CABELL
A contemporary of Zor, Cabell was left behind on Tirol to continue his research into the secrets of Protoculture while the Masters journeyed to Earth.

REM
Cabell's young assistant and student—a Robotech Master in training, determined to aid Cabell in uncovering the secrets held by The Flower Of Life.

REGENT
The leader of the Invid invasion of Tirol. The Regent is obsessed with destroying Fantoma and the civilization of the Robotech Masters who stole the precious Flower of Life from the Invid.

REGISS
Referred to in this issue as "insolent slime," the Regiss is in fact the Regent's wife, transformed by Protoculture to resemble Zor's race.

JACK BAKER
Orphaned during the First Robotech War, Jack is determined to become a member of the REF.

KAREN PENN
The daughter of Dr. Harry Penn, a member of Dr. Lang's research group. Her mother was killed during the First Robotech War and her father has forbid her to join the REF—an order she ignores.

CHAPTER ONE

TIROL, THE THIRD MOON OF FANTOMA.

THE HOMEWORLD OF THE ROBOTECH MASTERS.

A WORLD UNDER SIEGE.

HELP!

PLEASE... PLEASE...WE HAVE DONE NOTHING!

PHOOOM!

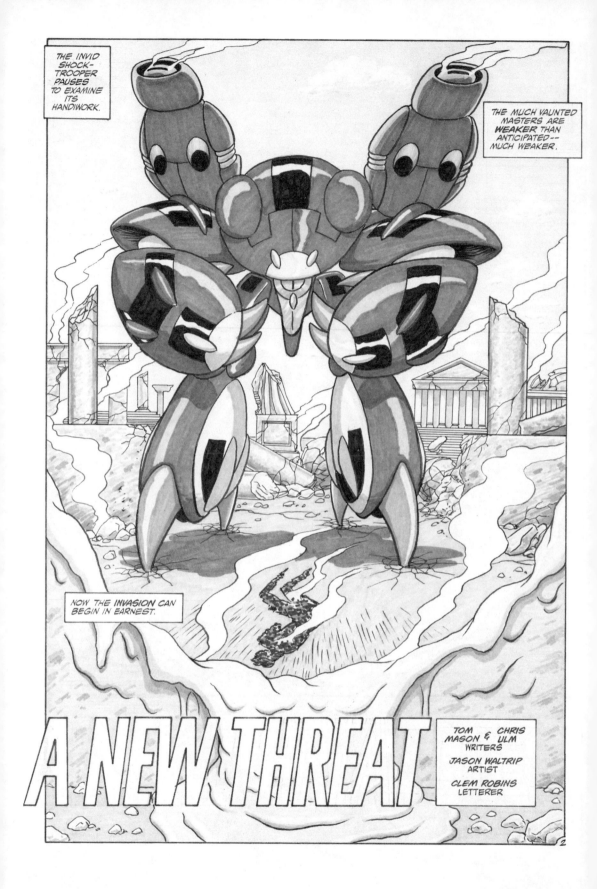

THE INVID
SHOCK-
TROOPER
PAUSES
TO EXAMINE
ITS
HANDIWORK.

THE MUCH VAUNTED
MASTERS ARE
WEAKER THAN
ANTICIPATED--
MUCH WEAKER.

NOW THE INVASION CAN
BEGIN IN EARNEST.

A NEW THREAT

TOM
MASON & CHRIS
ULM
WRITERS

JASON WALTRIP
ARTIST

CLEM ROBINS
LETTERER

2

LIGHT YEARS AWAY, ON THE GREEN PLANET OF EARTH, IN THE 21ST CENTURY.

IN THE WAR-TORN CITY OF MONUMENT, EARTH'S UNOFFICIAL CAPITAL CITY AND THE SEAT OF THE UNITED EARTH GOVERNMENT...

...A FATEFUL MISSION HAS BEGUN AFTER A NINE YEAR WAIT...

SHUTTLE LAUNCH FOR TAKE-OFF IN T-MINUS FIVE MINUTES AND COUNTING.

AS COMMANDER OF THE *ROBOTECH EXPEDITIONARY FORCE,* YOU MIGHT AGREE IT'S WORTH YOUR TIME.

THERE IS *ALWAYS* THE POTENTIAL FOR WAR WITH THE *ROBOTECH MASTERS.*

I HOPE WE CAN SETTLE OUR DIFFERENCES PEACEFULLY, BUT WE NEED A PLAN IF DIPLOMACY FAILS.

LOOK AT IT THIS WAY, DR. LANG. THE *SDF-3* IS LOADED WITH THE LATEST AND MOST POWERFUL MECHA WE'VE EVER DEVISED. IF THINGS GET HOT, WE SHOULD BE PREPARED FOR ANYTHING.

BESIDES, THE *SDF-3* LOOKS MORE LIKE A *ZENTRAEDI* SHIP NOW THAN WHEN WE FIRST FOUND IT ON THE ISLAND 20 YEARS AGO.

I WOULDN'T SAY IT LOOKS *MORE* ZENTRAEDI, BUT YOUR ENGINEERS HAVE CREATED A *VERY* INTERESTING FACSIMILE.

BREETAI HAS BEEN SUPERVISING THE RECONSTRUCTION.

I JUST HOPE THE *ROBOTECH MASTERS* WILL BE FOOLED BY OUR LITTLE MASQUERADE.

WHY WOULDN'T THEY? IT'S THE PERFECT PLAN.

IT'S *IRRELEVANT,* GENTLEMEN.

7

FIRST WE'VE GOT TO GET TO THEIR HOMEWORLD. WE DON'T KNOW IF THE *SDF-3* CAN EVEN FOLD INTO HYPER-SPACE, YET.

AND IF IT DOES, THERE'S NO GUARANTEE THAT WE'LL COME OUT WHERE WE WANT TO.

WE ARE ABOUT TO EMBARK ON A TRIP INTO THE UNKNOWN. A TRIP TO MEET OUR DESTINY HEAD ON...

TO FACE A NEW THREAT.

I JUST HOPE WE'RE PREPARED.

I HATE TO INTERRUPT, GENTLEMEN, BUT WE HAVE THE FACTORY SATELLITE ON *VISUAL*.

DR. LANG...COULD I SPEAK TO YOU FOR A SECOND?

WHAT IS IT, VINCE?

IT'S ABOUT VICE ADMIRAL HUNTER.

HE'S BEEN ACTING STRANGE LATELY. JEAN, MY WIFE, SAID HE DIDN'T SAY A *WORD* DURING HIS MEDICAL EXAMINATION.

IT'S AN IMPORTANT DAY FOR RICK. THE CULMINATION OF YEARS OF HARD WORK ON THE SDF-3.

"AND BESIDES, A MAN HAS A LOT TO THINK ABOUT BEFORE HE MARRIES AN ADMIRAL OF THE ROBOTECH DEFENSE FORCE."

I KNOW. AND I WISH CLAUDIA AND ROY HAD LIVED TO SEE THIS.

WE CAN'T LIVE IN THE PAST, VINCE. WE ALL MISS YOUR SISTER.

AND ROY FOKKER WAS LIKE A BROTHER TO RICK...

9

HEY--AREN'T WE FORGETTING SOMETHING?

WHAT, MAX?

WE'VE GOT TO GIVE OUR PAL THE BEST *BACHELOR PARTY* IN THE HISTORY OF THE *R.D.F.*!

IS THAT ALLOWED? I THOUGHT THERE WAS NO CIVILIAN LIFE ON THE REPAIR STATION.

THERE DIDN'T USED TO BE, BUT THINGS HAVE CHANGED SINCE COMMANDER RENO WAS OVERTHROWN.

"THE SHUTTLE IS ABOUT TO DOCK AT THE LANDING BAY, GEN. EDWARDS."

THANK YOU, BENSON, BUT I CAN SEE THAT MYSELF.

TELL ME, BENSON, WHAT DO YOU KNOW OF THE ILLUSTRIOUS COMMANDER HUNTER? QUICKLY!

WELL SIR, I KNOW HE WAS THE LEADER OF THE SKULL SQUADRON DURING THE WAR, THAT HE WAS THE COMMANDER OF THE RDF AFTER THE DESTRUCTION OF THE FIRST SUPERDIMENSIONAL FORTRESS...

...AND THAT HE'S ABOUT TO MARRY ADMIRAL LISA HAYES AND...

ENOUGH! YOU WILL DO NICELY, BENSON.

I ADMIRE A MAN WITH A GOOD MEMORY. IT WON'T BE LONG BEFORE WE SEE EXACTLY WHAT THE FAMOUS RICK HUNTER IS MADE OF.

IF HE'S ANYTHING LIKE HIS PAL FOKKER, IT SHOULDN'T BE TOO DIFFICULT TO PUT OUR PLAN INTO ACTION.

HOW DO YOU FIGURE THAT, SIR?

I'VE WAITED LONG TIME FOR JUST E RIGHT MOMENT TO EIZE CONTROL OF THE MILITARY.

I'VE STUDIED EVERY VARIABLE, AND IF WE PLAY OUR CARDS RIGHT...

AREN'T YOU FORGETTING THE ROBOTECH MASTERS? THEY COULD EASILY BECOME A PROBLEM.

JUST LEAVE EVERYTHING TO ME. WHEN THE TIME IS RIGHT I'LL DEAL WITH THEM ...OR WHATEVER ALIEN FORCE MIGHT BE IN MY WAY.

BUT RICK HUNTER COULD RUIN *EVERY-THING.*

IF I HAD MY WAY, HE'D STILL BE ON EARTH AND *I'D* BE IN CHARGE OF THIS MISSION. THAT'S WHY HE'S GOT TO BE TAKEN CARE OF *FIRST.*

THAT'S WHERE *YOU* COME IN.

ME, SIR?

I WANT YOU TO READ THIS AND STICK CLOSE TO HIM, FIND OUT ALL YOU CAN ABOUT THE WAY HE THINKS...THE WAY HE RESPONDS TO A GIVEN SITUATION.

HUNTER, R.

MANY PEOPLE HAVE TRIED TO GET THE BEST OF HUNTER, SIR, AND MOST...

HUNTER, R

AND MOST HAVE *FAILED!*

I'VE BEEN A *SOLDIER* LONGER THAN HUNTER'S BEEN ALIVE! AND I'LL *STILL* BE A SOLDIER LONG AFTER HE'S *DEAD!*

IS THAT CLEAR?

YES, SIR. *VERY* CLEAR. YOU CAN COUNT ON ME, SIR.

ON THE EMBATTLED HOMEWORLD OF THE ROBOTECH MASTERS.

THE SECOND WAVE OF INVID TROOPS PREPARE TO LEAVE THEIR CARRIERS.

THE **SHOCKTROOPERS** ARE THE CREAM OF THE INVID ASSAULT GROUPS.

WITHOUT THE PROTECTION OF THEIR GIANT WARRIOR CLONES, THE ZENTRAEDI, THE ROBOTECH MASTERS ARE **NO MATCH** FOR SUCH AS THESE.

THE WORLD OF TIROL IS **DOOMED.**

13

BLAAM!

ON THE OUTSKIRTS OF TOWN, THE REMAINING DEFENDERS ARE NO MATCH FOR THE INVID.

AN ADVANCED TECHNOLOGICAL FIGHTING FORCE THAT LIVES FOR COMBAT, THE INVID ARE MERCILESS.

CRUNCH

PHOOM

BWAAM!

NO QUARTER IS GIVEN TO THE OUT-GUNNED DEFENDERS.

BA-BOOOM!

NONE GIVEN IN RETURN.

THE INVID STORM TROOPERS *SWARM* FROM THE GENTLE SKY OF TIROL.

DISPENSING DESTRUCTION LIKE *RAINDROPS.*

AGE OLD MONUMENTS OF INCALCULABLE CULTURAL VALUE ARE BLASTED TO DUST WITH THE WAVE OF AN ARMORED PINCER.

BA-BOOM!

BOOM

BLAAM

BLAM

BLAM

A CITY THAT TOOK CENTURIES TO BUILD AND REFINE IS DESTROYED IN BUT A *FEW HOURS.*

THE FIGHTING ON THE SURFACE SOUNDS *INCREDIBLE.* WE'LL BE SAFE ONCE WE REACH THE CATACOMBS, REM.

WE HAVE ENOUGH PROVISIONS TO LAST US A WEEK.

RUMMBLE

A WEEK?

ARE YOU OUT OF YOUR MIND, CABELL? THESE INVID ARE HERE TO STAY!

THEY HAVE *DESTROYED* OUR WORLD! WE'RE *DOOMED!*

CALM DOWN, MY BOY. YOU'RE *UPSETTING* OUR LITTLE FRIENDS.

LET ME CARRY THEM.

YOU ARE A YOUNG *ROBOTECH MASTER,* REM. HAVE *PATIENCE.* WE WILL BE RESCUED.

THAT'S EASY FOR YOU TO SAY, CABELL. YOU'RE OLD. YOU'VE LIVED *YOUR* LIFE.

IF THE *INVID* FIND US, IT IS OF LITTLE CONCERN TO YOU.

KLIK!

BUT I AM *YOUNG*.

I *SHOULD* HAVE MY WHOLE LIFE *AHEAD* OF ME.

PRECISELY WHY YOU SHOULD *NEVER* SUCCUMB TO THE INVID.

YOU MUST RETAIN THE *COURAGE* OF A ROBOTECH MASTER IF WE ARE TO DEFEAT THEM.

ARE YOU SURE THEY WON'T FIND US HERE?

"NOT UNLESS THEY'VE LEARNED TO SEE THROUGH LEAD WALLS."

SNAK!

19

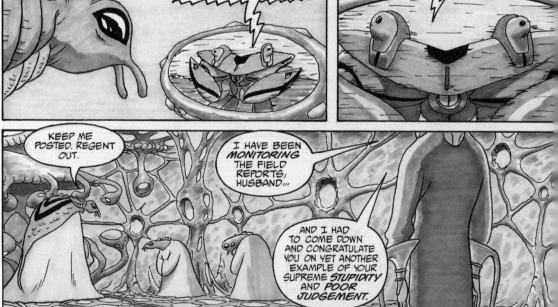

HOW *DARE* YOU! MY TROOPS HAVE KEPT OUR CIVILIZATION ALIVE WHILE WE MOUNTED THE CRUSADE TO RECAPTURE OUR STOLEN TREASURE.

IT IS OUR *LIFE'S BLOOD!* OUR FUTURE!

FURTHER CONVERSATION WITH YOU *BORES* ME.

I AM RETIRING TO MY CHAMBER TO MEDITATE. PERHAPS I WILL BE ABLE TO DETECT A CLUE AS TO THE WHEREABOUTS OF THE SEEDS WE SEEK.

WHATEVER I DO, IT CAN BE NO WORSE THAN *YOU,* MY FOOLHARDY HUSBAND.

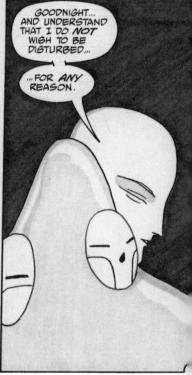

GOODNIGHT... AND UNDERSTAND THAT I DO *NOT* WISH TO BE DISTURBED...

...FOR *ANY* REASON.

NEXT: MORE NEW THREATS IN **PART II**

23

CHAPTER TWO

A NEW THREAT PART II

TOM MASON & CHRIS ULM - WRITERS / JOHN WALTRIP - ARTIST / CLEM ROBINS - LETTERER

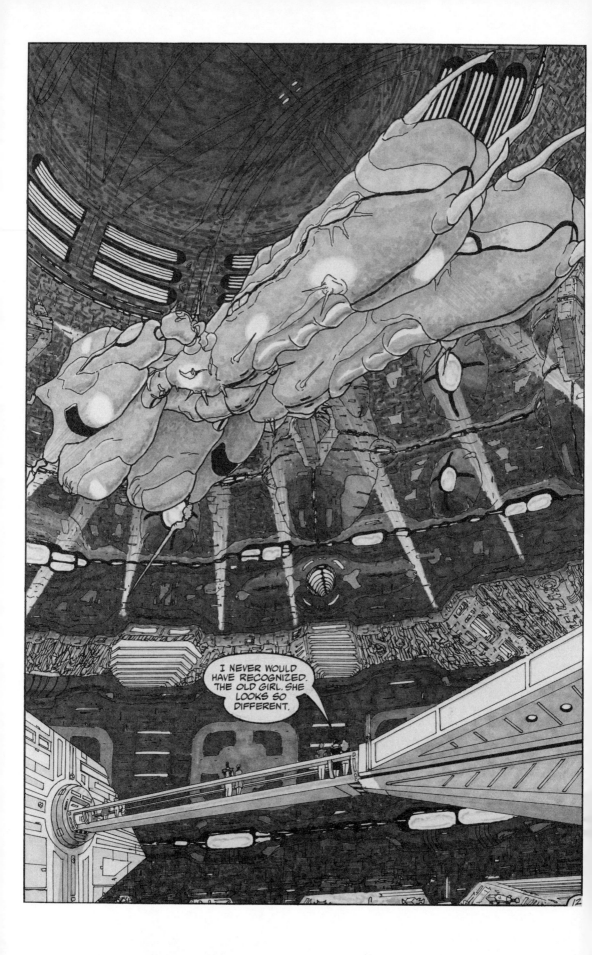

AND IF IT'S ALL THE SAME TO YOU, I WOULD LIKE TO HAVE *HIS* OPINION ON THE SAFETY OF THIS VESSEL DURING A JUMP THROUGH HYPER-SPACE.

EXEDORE'S RIGHT. I STILL REMEMBER WHAT HAPPENED WHEN THE SDF-1 MADE HER FIRST JUMP.

SHE TOOK *MACROSS CITY* WITH HER INTO DEEP SPACE!

THAT WILL *NEVER* HAPPEN AGAIN. NEVER. I CAN ASSURE YOU!

I STILL WILL NOT BE SATISFIED UNTIL I RECEIVE A *FULL REPORT* FROM COMMANDER BREETAI.

I AGREE. THIS MISSION IS TOO *VALUABLE* TO LEAVE *ANYTHING* TO CHANCE.

SOMEONE AS *BIG* AS *BREETAI* SHOULDN'T BE *TOO* HARD TO SPOT IN A PLACE LIKE THIS.

MAYBE HE FORGOT WE WERE COMING?

UNLIKELY. THAT'S *NOT* LIKE BREETAI.

14

SHORTLY.

IN THE OBSERVATION ROOM.

WE'VE GOT TO MAKE THIS FAST.

I HAVE A WEDDING TO ATTEND TO. PLEASE CONTINUE, EXEDORE.

THIRD MOON -TIROL

THANK YOU, RICK.

GENTLEMEN, YOU ACT AS THOUGH WE KNOW *NOTHING* ABOUT THE ROBOTECH MASTERS.

YOU WERE CREATED BY THEM AS AN EXPERIMENT IN BIO-GENETIC ENGINEERING, AM I RIGHT, EXEDORE?

CORRECT, COLONEL WOLFF. THE ZENTRAEDI SERVED THE ROBOTECH MASTERS AS WARRIORS FOR MANY YEARS.

AS I HAVE TOLD THE ROBOTECH RESEARCH CENTER AND THE UNITED EARTH GOVERNMENT REPEATEDLY, THE MAJORITY OF THE POPULATION ON THE MASTER'S HOMEWORLD --THE THIRD MOON OF FANTOMA--ARE NOT ALL TOGETHER DIFFERENT FROM YOU MICRONIANS.

WE MAY *NOT* HAVE TO GO TO WAR WITH THEM AFTER WE'VE HAD A CHANCE TO TALK AND FIND OUT WHAT THEY WANT.

I HOPE SO, EXEDORE. FOR *ALL* OUR SAKES.

17.

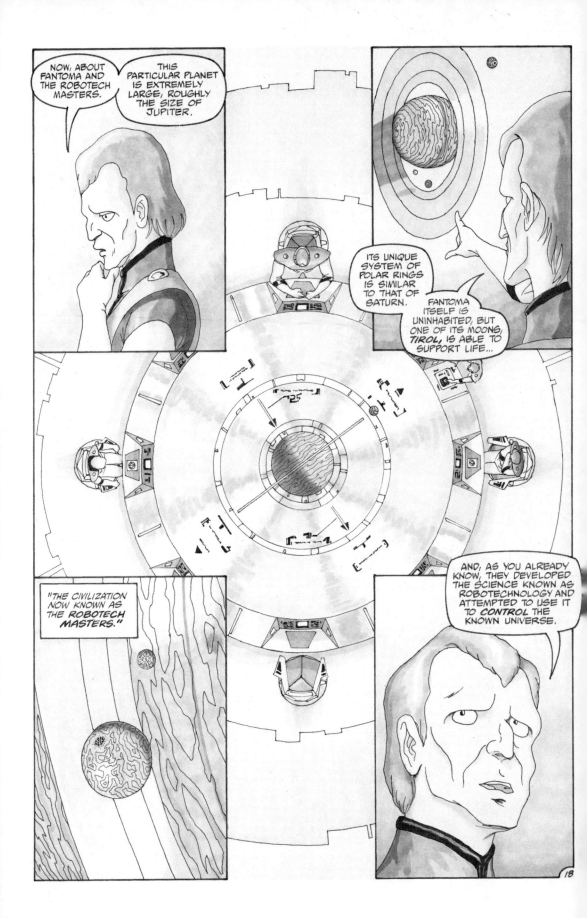

ARE THEY AS *BIG* AS THE ZENTRAEDI?

A GOOD QUESTION, BUT NO, THEY ARE HUMAN-SIZED. WE'VE ALWAYS CALLED THEM MICRONIANS.

THEN *WHY* DID THEY MAKE THE ZENTRAEDI SO LARGE?

IT DOESN'T SEEM VERY INTELLIGENT TO CREATE A RACE *MORE* POWERFUL THAN THE RULING PARTY.

THEY HAD THEIR REASONS. ORIGINALLY WE WERE CREATED TO *MINE ORE* ON FANTOMA.

MA SYSTEM

TIROL
3rd moon

SO THE GREAT ZENTRAEDI WERE NOTHING MORE THAN *OVERSIZED DITCH-DIGGERS!*

WHAT A *JOKE.*

THEN THE *GRAVITY* OF FANTOMA PROBABLY DICTATED THE *SIZE* OF THE ORIGINAL ZENTRAEDI.

MEANING NO DIS-RESPECT, "FLYBOY," BUT HOW WOULD *YOU* KNOW THAT?

19

IT'S VERY SIMPLE. A PERSON OUR SIZE WOULD BE CRUSHED BY THE GRAVITATIONAL FORCES OF A PLANET AS LARGE AS FANTOMA.

AN EXCELLENT DEDUCTION, RICK. AND *VERY* ACCURATE.

LOOK, I DON'T *CARE* WHY THE ZENTRAEDI WERE CREATED.

THERE ARE ONLY A HANDFUL OF THEM LEFT, AND BY THE END OF THIS MISSION, THEY'LL PROBABLY BE *DEAD* ANYWAY.

WHAT I WANT TO *KNOW* IS WHY THEY HAVE TO PARTICIPATE IN THESE *BRIEFING* SESSIONS?

STRONG WORDS, BENSON. FOR STARTERS, THE ZENTRAEDI HAVE *FIRST* HAND KNOWLEDGE OF THE *ROBOTECH MASTERS* --KNOWLEDGE THAT WE MUST HAVE TO STAY ALIVE.

SECONDLY, BOTH BREETAI AND EXEDORE ARE *FRIENDS* OF MINE. WITHOUT THEIR HELP DURING THE WAR, *NONE* OF US WOULD BE HERE TODAY.

AND FINALLY...

I DON'T RECALL ANYBODY ASKING *YOU* TO ATTEND.

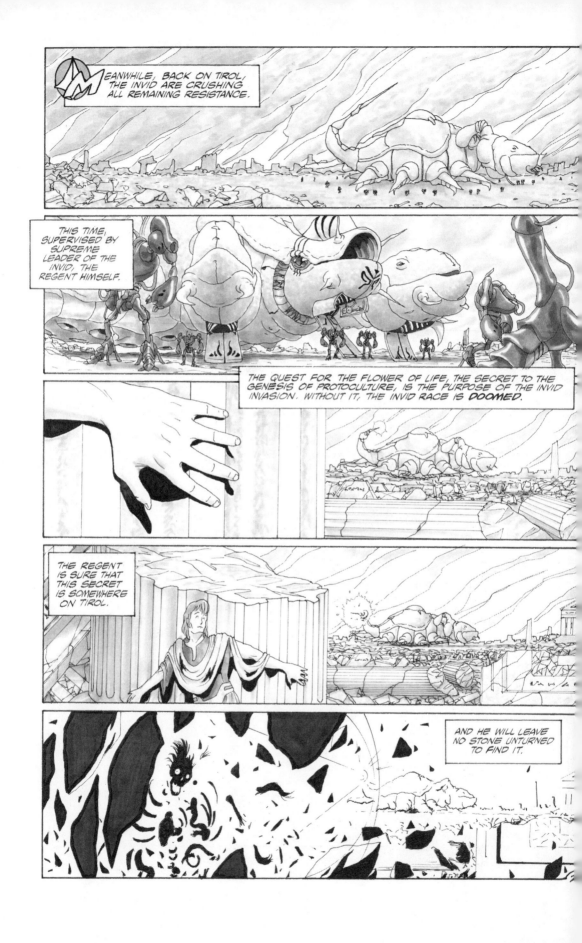

MEANWHILE, BACK ON TIROL, THE INVID ARE CRUSHING ALL REMAINING RESISTANCE.

THIS TIME, SUPERVISED BY SUPREME LEADER OF THE INVID, THE REGENT HIMSELF.

THE QUEST FOR THE FLOWER OF LIFE, THE SECRET TO THE GENESIS OF PROTOCULTURE, IS THE PURPOSE OF THE INVID INVASION. WITHOUT IT, THE INVID RACE IS *DOOMED.*

THE REGENT IS SURE THAT THIS SECRET IS SOMEWHERE ON TIROL.

AND HE WILL LEAVE NO STONE UNTURNED TO FIND IT.

THE CENTRAL TEMPLE OF THE ROBOTECH MASTERS. IT IS HERE THAT THE REGENT HOPES TO DISCOVER THE SECRETS OF ROBOTECHNOLOGY.

INSIDE THE IMPERIAL LANDCRUISER...

SOON THE SECRETS OF PROTOCULTURE WILL BE OURS! NOW THE REGISS WILL SEE THAT INVADING TIROL WAS NO MISTAKE!

RELEASE THE ENFORCERS!

ENFORCERS--THE ELITE POLICE FORCE OF THE INVID, SINGLE-MINDED SENTRIES WITH ONLY ONE THING ON THEIR MINDS--

FINDING THE FLOWER OF LIFE.

23

BACK ABOARD THE ROBOTECH REPAIR FACTORY, RICK HUNTER PACKS HIS PERSONAL EFFECTS FOR THE JOURNEY AHEAD.

DO YOU NEED ANY HELP, SIR?

HELLO, VINCE. DID YOU GET THE PROGRESS REPORT FROM MAX?

HE SAYS THAT THE SELECTION FOR THE ROBOTECH EXPEDITIONARY FORCE IS GOING FASTER THAN WE HOPED. ALMOST 70 PERCENT OF THE TROOPS ARE ASSIGNED.

AND IF ALL GOES WELL, HE SHOULD BE FINISHED NO LATER THAN WEDNESDAY.

SOUNDS LIKE EVERYTHING IS MOVING ALONG. WE SHOULD MAKE OUR LAUNCH WINDOW WITHOUT INCIDENT.

THE ONLY THING I'M WORRIED ABOUT IS GEN. EDWARDS.

I BELIEVE HE HAS PLANS OF HIS OWN. IT'S NOTHING I CAN PUT MY FINGER ON...

WHAT ABOUT HIM?

CAN YOU BACK THESE ALLEGATIONS WITH ANY HARD FACTS?

NO, SIR, ONLY HEARSAY. YOU'VE BEEN BUSY WITH THE LAUNCH AND THE WEDDING, SIR, YOU HAVEN'T HEARD THE SCUTTLEBUTT...

24

AND I HEARD ABOUT THE LITTLE CONFRONTATION YOU HAD WITH HIS AIDE, BENSON, IN THE OBSERVATION ROOM.

UNLESS YOU HAVE *EVIDENCE*, VINCE, I DON'T WANT TO HEAR ABOUT IT. THIS MISSION WILL BE TOUGH ENOUGH WITHOUT A *DIVIDED* CREW.

DISMISSED.

ROY FOKKER OFTEN WARNED ME ABOUT EDWARDS AND HIS SELF-SERVING ALLEGIANCES.

FIRST DURING THE *GLOBAL CIVIL WAR*, THEN WITH LISA'S FATHER, THE ADMIRAL, AND THEN THE *GRAND CANNON* PROJECT.

AND AS LEADER OF THE GHOST SQUADRON, HE'S BUILT UP A PRETTY SUBSTANTIAL POWER BASE.

VINCE DID SEEM GENUINELY WORRIED. EVEN WITHOUT *FACTS*, THERE MAY BE *SOMETHING* TO WHAT HE'S HEARD.

REF COMM
PERSONNEL QUARTER
ADMIRAL
LISA HAYES

I'LL KEEP AN EYE ON HIM.

AND MY OTHER ONE ON THE MISSION.

25

AND ANOTHER ONE ON LISA.

IF ONLY I KNEW WHERE TO GET A THIRD EYE.

OH MY.

HELLO, STRANGER. LONG TIME NO SEE.

WELL, ER, IT'S BAD LUCK TO SEE YOUR FIANCE IN HER WEDDING DRESS BEFORE THE WEDDING.

DON'T BE SUPERSTITIOUS!

BESIDES, I WASN'T IN MY DRESS, JUST BEHIND IT. SO THERE!

ATTEN...SHUN!

WHAT?

IT'S TIME YOU REALIZED WHO'S IN COMMAND AROUND HERE, VICE-ADMIRAL HUNTER.

NOW, HOW ABOUT A KISS?

I JUST HOPE WE'RE MAKING THE RIGHT DECISION, LISA. LEAVING THE EARTH DEFENSELESS WHILE WE GO OFF CHASING SOME DREAM. THE MORE I THINK ABOUT IT, THE MORE APPREHENSIVE I GET.

THE RDF IS STRONG. UNITED UNDER GENERAL LEONARD AND ROLF EMERSON, THEY'LL BE ABLE TO HANDLE THINGS WHILE WE'RE GONE.

26

"AND OUR WEDDING... ON THE EVE OF THE LAUNCH. IT'S ALL HAPPENING TOO FAST."

"WHAT DO YOU MEAN, FAST? YOU'VE HAD NINE YEARS TO PREPARE FOR BOTH THE MISSION AND OUR MARRIAGE!"

"OH, RICK, OUR LIVES ARE JUST ABOUT TO BEGIN!"

NEXT ISSUE:
PREPARATIONS!

27

CHAPTER THREE

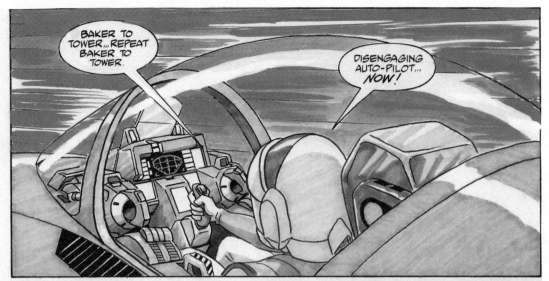

PREPARATIONS

TOM MASON & CHRIS ULM -WRITERS / JASON WALTRIP -ARTIST / CLEM ROBINS -LETTERER

SUBJECT ELIMINATED. TEST IS CONCLUDED.

PLEASE EXIT SIMULATOR.

DISENGAGE HOLOGRAM. PREPARE FOR NEXT CANDIDATE...

CADET BAKER, PLEASE ENTER THE DEBRIEFING ROOM FOR FINAL TEST SCORES AND COMPUTER ANALYSIS.

YOU'VE GOT TO ADMIT IT, RICK--HE'S GOT A LOT OF STYLE ...AND COURAGE!

FOOLHARDINESS IS MORE LIKE IT, MAX. HE GOT US BOTH KILLED.

CADET BAKER IS IN THE STAGING ROOM, SIR.

THANKS, DAVIS. WE'LL BE RIGHT THERE.

SHORTLY...

MILKY WAY CENTRAL

QUITE A *SHOW* YOU GAVE US, BAKER!

WELL, SIR, I THOUGHT...

IN THE *FIRST* PLACE, YOU WERE TOO QUICK TO DROP FROM AUTO-PILOT, DISOBEYING A DIRECT ORDER...

YOUR *GRANDSTANDING* COULD HAVE COST THE *LIVES* OF THE ENTIRE SQUAD. AND FINALLY...

YOU DIDN'T EVEN MANAGE TO RESCUE ME!

YOU MAY KNOW HOW TO PILOT A VERITECH FIGHTER, BAKER, BUT YOU'VE GOT TO LEARN *CONTROL.*

YOUR SKILLS ARE *NOTHING* IF YOU END UP *DEAD.*

DISMISSED.

YES, SIR, I APPRECIATE THE ADMIRAL'S INPUT.

9

MAYBE YOU SHOULDN'T HAVE BEEN SO ROUGH ON HIM.

I KNOW.

BUT THE *LOOK* ON HIS FACE WAS *PRICELESS*.

HE'S GOT ALL THE SKILLS, BUT HE'S GOT TO LEARN TO FOLLOW ORDERS, TO BE A *TEAM PLAYER*.

KIND OF REMINDS ME OF A CERTAIN YOUNG AMATEUR PILOT *I* ONCE HEARD ABOUT...

A YOUNG *HOTHEAD* FLYBOY NAMED HUNTER.

HUH?

YOU HEARD ME, COMMANDER.

FUNNY, I WAS JUST THINKING THE SAME THING, MAX.

C'MON. LET'S GET SOMETHING TO EAT BEFORE WE WATCH THE REST OF THE RECRUITS. BEING *KILLED* GIVES ME AN APPETITE.

I DON'T WANT TO HEAR TALK LIKE THAT SO CLOSE TO THE WEDDING, LADIES.

WELL, WHAT DO YOU THINK?

I HAVE TO ADMIT IT, LISA, IT WAS *WORTH* THE WAIT!

NOT BAD...ADMIRAL. BUT HOW WILL IT HANDLE *HYPER-SPACE TRAVEL?*

DO YOU THINK *RICK* WILL LIKE IT?

. I THINK HE'LL LIKE IT VERY MUCH, LISA.

OH, LISA, I WANT SO MUCH FOR *BYGONES* TO BE *BYGONES*.

ME TOO. IT'S BEEN A *LONG* TIME.

YOU HAVEN'T CHANGED A BIT.

I JUST GOT OFF THE SHUTTLE AND I CAME BY TO SEE IF THERE WAS ANYTHING I COULD DO TO HELP WITH THE WEDDING.

IF YOU'LL *LET* ME.

DON'T BE SILLY, MINMEI. OF *COURSE* YOU CAN HELP.

OH, TO HAVE THE BEAUTIFUL SINGER *LYNN MINMEI* IN MY SHOP. SUCH A *DEAL*.

WHERE IS A *PHOTOGRAPHER?* I HOPE SOMEBODY SAW HER COME IN.

FACTORY TAILORING
UNIFORMS MINIATURIZED ALTERATIONS

WAIT UNTIL I TELL MY *WIFE!*

REMEMBER THE *FIRST* TIME WE SET FOOT ON THE FACTORY?

AFTER *LIBERATING* IT FROM COMMANDER RENO?

OF COURSE. IT'S SOMETHING I'LL *NEVER* FORGET.

THAT AND BABY *DANA'S* PART IN THE OPERATION.

IT'S A *SHAME* WE HAVE TO LEAVE HER BEHIND THIS TIME.

SHE'LL BE FINE.

HOW ARE *YOU* HOLDING UP? THE *WEDDING'S* IN JUST A FEW DAYS.

I'M OKAY. A LITTLE NERVOUS, MAYBE.

BUT IT'S NOT THE WEDDING, IT'S THE MISSION.

I CAN'T HELP THINKING WE'VE TAKEN ON *TOO MUCH* THIS TIME.

15

I HOPE YOU'RE NOT GOING TO START IN AGAIN ABOUT HOW YOU'RE THE YOUNGEST ADMIRAL IN THE FORCE...

AND HOW *UNDESERVING* YOU ARE.

THE BEST AND THE BRIGHTEST, THAT'S ME.

I HOPE I'M NOT *DISTURBING* YOU, ADMIRAL?

WHAT'S ON YOUR *MIND*, EDWARDS?

I JUST WANTED TO WISH YOU *GOOD LUCK,* HUNTER.

WHAT DO YOU MEAN BY *THAT?*

WHY, THE *WEDDING,* OF COURSE.

ADMIRAL HAYES'S DAUGHTER...

THE *IRONY* OF IT, I MEAN.

NO *LOVE* LOST BETWEEN YOU AND HIM BACK THEN, WAS THERE?

OH, I'M SORRY, ADMIRAL. I GUESS YOU DON'T LIKE TO *REMEMBER* THOSE DAYS.

ANYWAY, *GOOD LUCK* TO YOU. YOU TOO, STERLING.

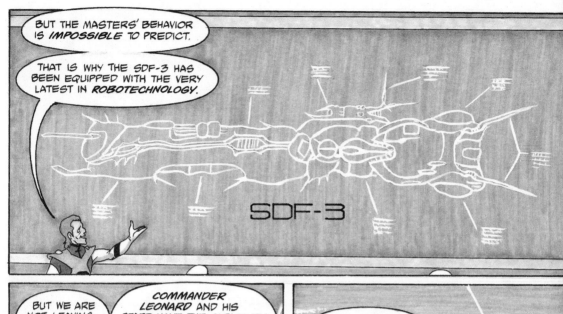

BUT THE MASTERS' BEHAVIOR IS *IMPOSSIBLE* TO PREDICT.

THAT IS WHY THE SDF-3 HAS BEEN EQUIPPED WITH THE VERY LATEST IN *ROBOTECHNOLOGY*.

SDF-3

BUT WE ARE NOT LEAVING THE EARTH UNPROTECTED.

COMMANDER LEONARD AND HIS STAFF HAVE THE CAPABILITY TO REPEL *ANY* INVASION FORCE, AND SINCE THE PLANET IS NOT CURRENTLY THREATENED WE ...

I'M NOT AS OPTIMISTIC AS THE *AMBASSADOR*.

SMACK!

THE DEPARTURE OF THE SDF-3 *AND* ITS WEAPONRY WILL LEAVE THE EARTH *VULNERABLE* TO ATTACK!

THE FACTORY SATELLITE'S A *USELESS* SHELL! WE'VE BEEN *STRIPPED* CLEAN!

I THINK YOU'RE BEING A BIT *PARANOID*, COMMANDER.

WHAT ATTACK? FROM *WHERE*? FROM *WHOM*?

FOR ALL WE KNOW, THERE MAY BE A FLEET OF YOUR *ZENTRAEDI* SHIPS OUT THERE, JUST *WAITING* FOR US TO DROP OUR GUARD.

THAT WILL BE *ENOUGH*, GENTLEMEN.

ALARMIST TALK IS OF NO USE TO *ANY* OF US.

VERY WELL, "GENTLEMEN." I'VE HAD MY SAY.

BUT MARK MY WORDS, ONCE THE SDF-3 LEAVES ORBIT, I WON'T BE ABLE TO DEFEND THIS PLANET AGAINST AN INVASION OF *DUCKS* AND *BUNNIES*.

19

THE PRESS CONFERENCE IS BEING CARRIED *LIVE* AROUND THE WORLD, SIR.

AND TO LUNA BASE, SPACE STATION LIBERTY, AND THE FACTORY SATELLITE.

COMMANDER LEONARD IS...

COMMANDER LEONARD IS *OVERPLAYING* HIS ROLE, BENSON.

BUT IT WILL HAVE THE DESIRED *EFFECT*, NONETHELESS.

THE *SOUTHERN CROSS* WILL EVENTUALLY GAIN THE UPPER HAND. *LAZLO ZAND* WILL SEE TO THAT, IF NECESSARY.

CLICK!

AND *SENATOR MORAN* WILL ASCEND TO THE SEAT WE'VE BEEN *GROOMING* HIM FOR.

BUT IT'S A PITY WE'LL HAVE TO MISS SOME OF THE *PROCEEDINGS,* BENSON.

WE'VE SET THESE PLANS INTO MOTION AND SOME OF THEM WILL REACH *FRUITION* WHILE WE'RE ON TIROL.

BUT THE *REWARDS* WILL BE WAITING FOR US ON OUR RETURN.

RIGHT NOW, I'VE GOT MORE *IMMEDIATE* SCORES TO SETTLE, BENSON.

SOME THAT GO BACK MORE THAN *TWENTY* YEARS.

21

THAT DEVIOUS LITTLE ALIEN, EXEDORE, HAS THE SUPREME COUNCIL *EATING* OUT OF HIS MICRONIZED HAND!

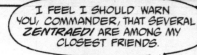

I FEEL I SHOULD WARN YOU, COMMANDER, THAT SEVERAL *ZENTRAEDI* ARE AMONG MY CLOSEST FRIENDS.

THAT'S *YOUR* PROBLEM, EMERSON.

AND IF THIS IS A *DIPLOMATIC* MISSION, WHY ARE THEY *ARMING* THE SDF-3 WITH EVERY ROBOTECH *WEAPONS* SYSTEM WE'VE DEVELOPED?

GUNBOAT DIPLOMACY, THEY USED TO CALL IT, COMMANDER.

BREETAI AND EXEDORE *BOTH* CLAIM NO KNOWLEDGE OF WHAT WEAPONS THE ROBOTECH MASTERS MIGHT *NOW* POSSESS.

WELL, SOMETHING *STINKS* HERE, MAJOR, AND I INTEND TO FIND OUT EXACTLY WHO, OR WHAT, IT IS.

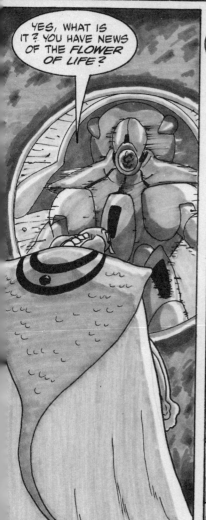

HAPTER FOUR

JASON WALTRIP '88

THE INORGANICS

TOM MASON & CHRIS ULM -WRITERS / JOHN WALTRIP-ARTIST / CLEM ROBINS-LETTERE...

IGHT YEARS AWAY, ABOARD THE ROBOTECH FACTORY SATELLITE.

I JUST DON'T KNOW.

I'M GAMBLING EVERY MEMBER OF THE ROBOTECH EXPEDITIONARY FORCE THAT THE MASTERS CAN BE *NEGOTIATED* WITH.

IF I'M WRONG, THEIR *BLOOD* WILL BE ON MY HANDS.

WATCHING BAKER IN THE SIMULATOR MADE ME REALIZE HOW MUCH I *ENVY* HIM.

HE'S IRRESPONSIBLE. *IMPULSIVE.*

THE WAY *I* USED TO BE.

"AND LISA.

"COMMAND COMES SO *EASY* TO HER.

5

AS YOU HAVE NO **DOUBT** HEARD, I HAVE RETURNED TO **OPTERA**.

UPON YOUR ARRIVAL, WE SHALL DISCUSS YOUR MOST RECENT FAILURES *AND* MY PLANS TO **CORRECT** THEM.

CLICK!

HOW LONG AGO DID SHE LEAVE?

LESS THAN A QUARTER OF A REVOLUTION. SHALL I GO **AFTER** HER?

NO. THE FARTHER AWAY SHE IS, THE **BETTER** I LIKE IT.

PREPARE THE ARMADA FOR THE RETURN TO OPTERA.

I'LL BE IN THE LAB.

I DO NOT WISH TO BE *DISTURBED*.

9

OBSIM! *REPORT!*

HELLO, MY LORD. IT IS *GOOD* TO SEE YOU AGAIN.

OH, SHUT UP. I WEARY OF SMALL TALK. I NEED *INFORMATION.*

AS MY CHIEF SCIENTIST, WHAT HAVE YOU *LEARNED* OF THIS WRETCHED PLANET?

IS THERE *ANYTHING* OF USE HERE?

ALAS, THERE IS NOTHING ON THIS WORLD FOR US, MY LORD.

NO TRACE OF THE FLOWER OF LIFE.

AND THE REMAINING INHABITANTS ARE A PITIFUL LOT--EITHER TOO OLD OR TOO SICK FOR SLAVE LABOR.

YES, I MET WITH SEVERAL OF THEM EARLIER TODAY.

NOW, COME WITH ME, OBSIM. WE HAVE *MUCH* TO DISCUSS.

YOUR WORK HERE HAS JUST *BEGUN.*

9

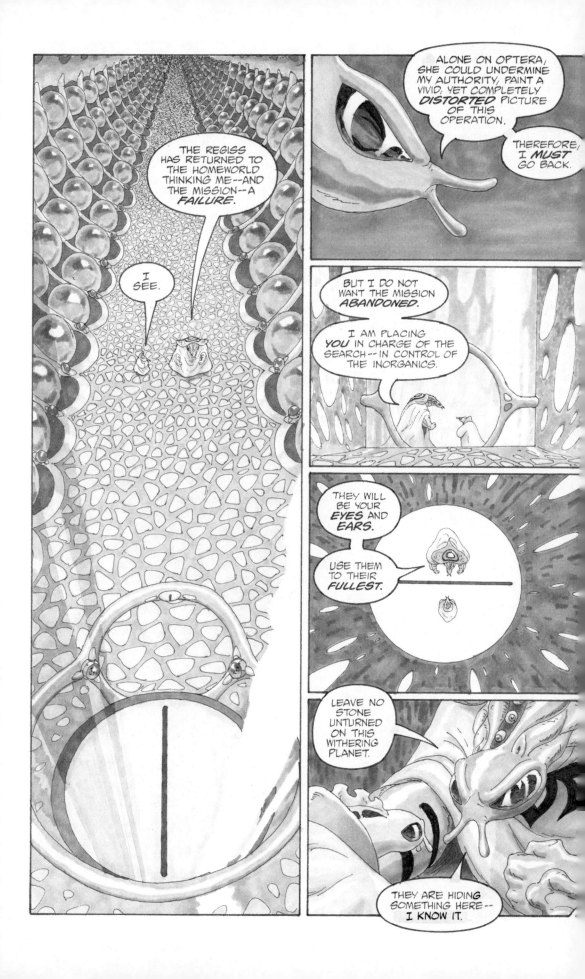

13

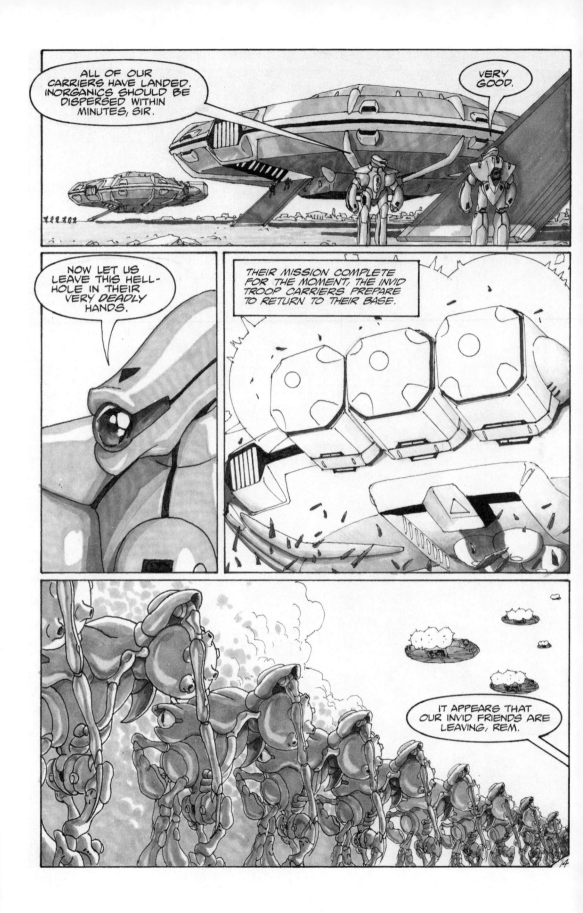

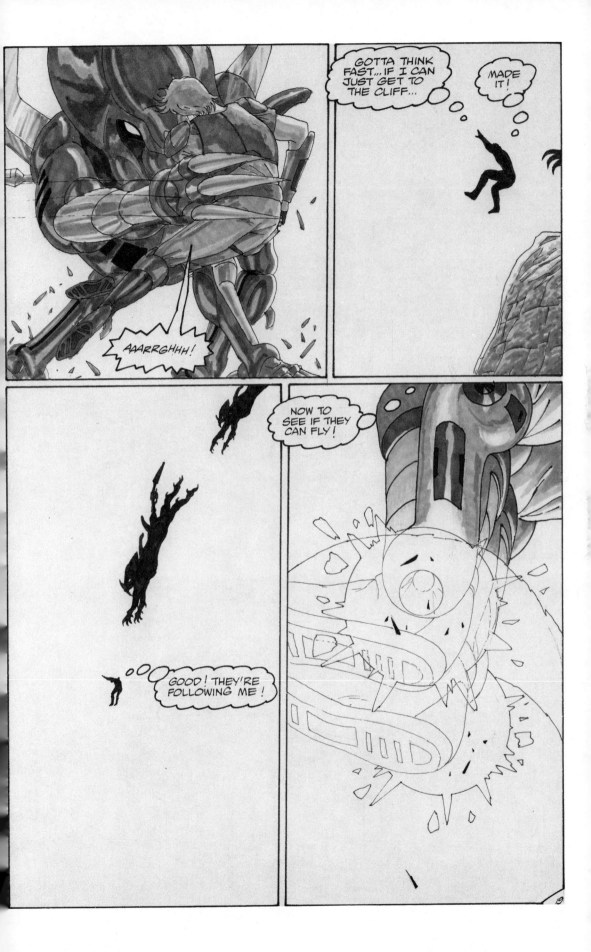

NEXT: **WAR TOYS**

22

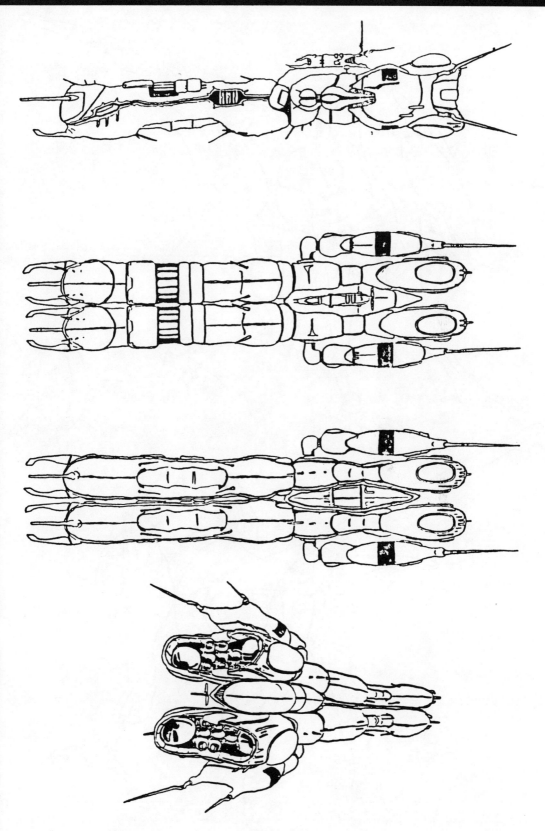

SDF-3

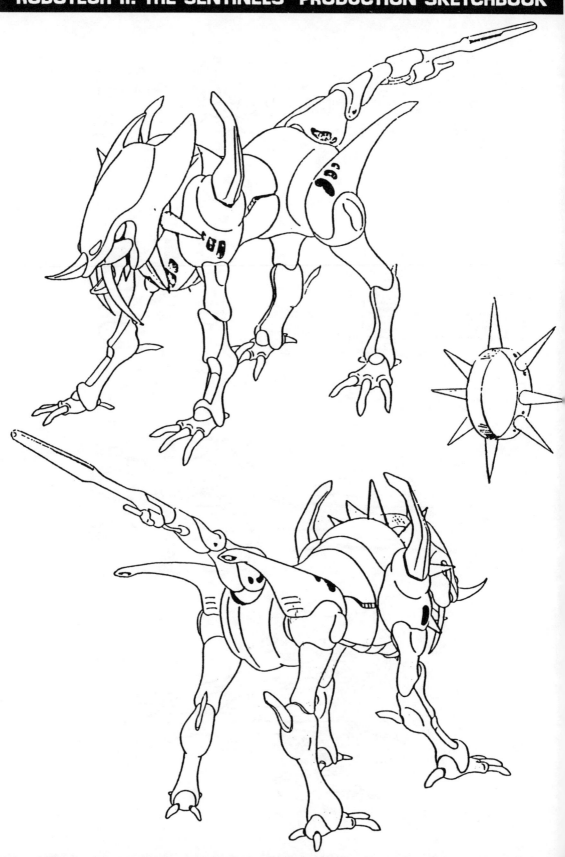

INVID HELLCAT

THE CITY OF TIROLIA

POLLINATORS

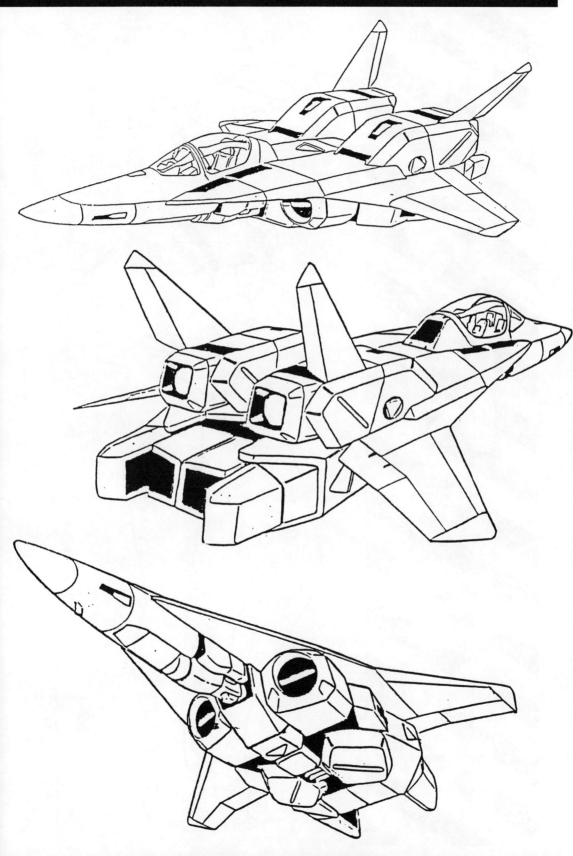

VERITECH ALPHA FIGHTER

LYNN MINMEI

ALSO AVAILABLE FROM MALIBU GRAPHICS

ABBOTT & COSTELLO
The Classic Comics Graphic Novel $17.00

BLADE OF SHURIKEN
#2-3,5 $1.00ea

BLIND FEAR
Sherlock Holmes returns! All new!
#1-3 $2.50ea

BUSHIDO
#1-4 $2.50ea

CAPTAIN HARLOCK
#1 $3.00

CHARLIE CHAN
#1-6 $2.50ea

CHINA SEA
Graphic Novel
From the creator of *Elflord*.
$7.00

COSMIC HEROES
Buck Rogers, 25th Century A.D. returns to comics in this monthly collection of the classic strip from the '30s.
#1-4, 6, 8 $2.50ea

CRIME CLASSICS
The Shadow returns
#1, 3-12 $2.50ea

DARK WOLF
(Mini-Series)
#1 $6.00
#2-4 $3.00ea
(Regular Series)
#1 $3.00 #2-4, 6-13 $2.50ea
Annual #1 $3.00
Dark Wolf Collection $8.00

DINOSAURS FOR HIRE
#1 (2nd print), #2-8 $2.50ea
Fall Classic #1 $3.00
Guns N'Lizards Graphic Novel $7.00

DRAGONFORCE
#5-10 $2.50ea
Chronicles #1-3 $3.50ea

EDGAR ALLAN POE
The Pit And The Pendulum $2.50
Mask Of Red Death $2.50
Rue Morgue $2.50
Black Cat $2.50

ELFLORD
#23-31 $2.50ea

EX-MUTANTS
(Original Series)
#1(Signed by Ron Lim) $10.00 ea
#6-10 $2.50ea

EX-MUTANTS: The Shattered Earth Chronicles
All new!
#1 $3.00
#2-10 $2.50ea
Annual #1 $3.00
Pin-Up Book #1 $3.00

FIFTIES TERROR
Pre-Code horror from the '50s.
#1-4, 6 $2.50ea

FIST OF GOD
#2-4 $2.50ea

FRANKENSTEIN
#1-3 $2.50ea

FRIGHT
#1-2,4-12 $2.50ea
#3 (Elm Street cover) $3.00

GUN FURY
#1-9 $2.50ea
#1 (Signed) $5.00

HEADLESS HORSEMAN
#1-2 $2.50ea

HOWL
#1-2 $2.50ea

HUMAN GARGOYLES
#1-4 $2.50ea

JAKE THRASH
The Complete Saga (80 pages) $4.50

KIKU SAN
#1-6 $2.50ea

LEATHER & LACE
#1-3 (Over 18 Only--state age when ordering) $3.00ea
#2-3 (General) $2.50ea

NEW HUMANS Shattered Earth
#2-15 $2.50ea
Annual #1 $3.50

NINJA HIGH SCHOOL
Ben Dunn
#6-14 $2.50ea
#1 (60 pp) $3.50
#2-3, 3 1/2, 4 $2.50ea
Graphic Novel $9.00
Graphic Novel (signed) $15.00

PRIVATE EYES
The Saint returns.
#1-3 $2.50ea
#4 (60 pp) $3.50
#5 (60 pp) $3.50

RIPPER
(shipped sealed because of violence)
#1 $3.00

ROBIN HOOD
#1-2 $2.50ea

ROBOTECH II: THE SENTINELS
#1 (2nd printing)
#2-9 $2.50ea
Wedding Special #1-2 $2.50ea
Full color poster $6.95

ROBOTECH II: THE SENTINELS The Malcontent Uprisings
#1-2 $2.50ea

SCARLET IN GASLIGHT Graphic Novel
Sherlock Holmes Vs. Dracula $8.00

SCIMIDAR
#1-2 $2.50ea
Book II #1 $6.00 (first printing)
Book II #1 (2nd printing) $2.75
Book II #2-4 $3.00ea

SHATTERED EARTH
Tales of the Ex-Mutants Universe
#1-5, 7-9 $2.50ea

SHERLOCK HOLMES
The classic strip from the '50s collected for the first time.
#1 $3.00
2-16 $2.50ea
Casebooks #1-2 $2.50ea

SHURIKEN: COLD STEEL
#1-2 $1.50ea
#3 $2.50

SHURIKEN TEAM-UP
#1 $1.00

SOLO EX-MUTANTS
#5-6 $2.50ea

SPICY DETECTIVE STORIES
The spiciest detective fiction of the '30s, complete with original illustrations.
$8.00

SPICY TALES
Bondage, Murder, and Seduction from the '30s.
#1, 5-12 $3.00ea

TEAM: NIPPON
#1-5 $2.50ea

THREE STOOGES
Graphic Novel:
The Knuckleheads Return $17.00

TIGER-X
Original series
#1, 3 $2.50ea
Book II #1 $2.50

TORRID AFFAIRS
'50s romance.
#1-2 $2.50ea
#3 (60 pp) $3.50
#4 (60 pp) $3.50

TROUBLE WITH GIRLS
#3 $4.00ea
#9, 11-14 $2.50ea
Graphic Novel Volume One $9.00
V2 #5-7 $2.50ea

TWILIGHT AVENGER
#1,3, 5-7 $2.50ea

VAMPYRES
#1-4 $2.50ea

VERDICT
#1-4 $1.00ea

VICTIMS
#1-5 $2.50ea

VIDEO CLASSICS
Here he comes to save the day--
Mighty Mouse!
#1-2 (60pp) $3.50ea

WALKING DEAD
All new Zombie Horror by Jim Somerville
#1-2 $2.50ea

WARLOCK 5
#16-22 $2.50ea
Book II #1-3 $2.50ea

WARLOCKS
#1 (Special Edition-40 pages) $3.00
#2-8 $2.50ea

WAR OF THE WORLDS
The Aliens have landed!
#1-4 $2.50ea

WEREWOLF AT LARGE
All new horror!
#1-3 $2.50ea

WILD KNIGHTS Shattered Earth
#1 $3.00
#2-10 $2.50ea

Note:
Minimum
Order--
5 Books.

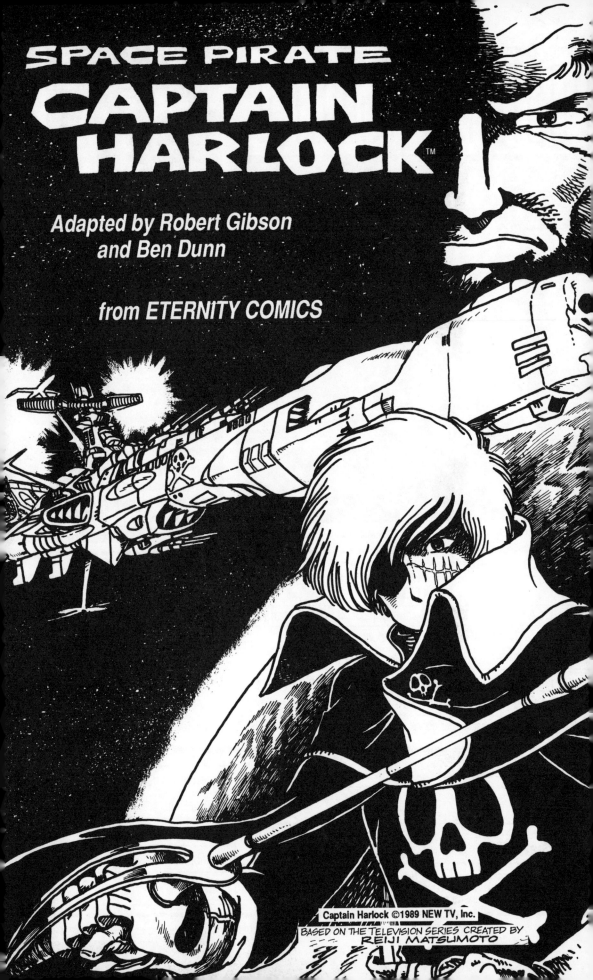

NINJA HIGH SCHOOL

Created,
Written, and
Illustrated by
BEN DUNN
Every Month From
ETERNITY COMICS
NINJA HIGH SCHOOL is trademarked
and copyright ©1989 Ben Dunn.

ROBOTECH II
THE SENTINELS ™

ROBOTECH II: THE SENTINELS ™
Adapted by
Tom Mason & Chris Ulm
Illustrated by
Jason Waltrip & John Waltrip

ROBOTECH II: THE SENTINELS — THE MALCONTENT UPRISINGS
Written by Bill Spangler
Illustrated by Michael Ling

TWO TITLES EVERY MONTH FROM

ETERNITY COMICS

Hello, Out There!

Regrettably, comics aren't a social activity. We don't get a chance to meet our readers as often as we would like. We can't invite you over for pizza and soda and classic movies on the VCR.

But, we would like to get to know you. We want to know who you are, what you're like, and what you think of our on-going efforts to bring you better comics day after day. Please take a minute and fill out the following questionaire. It is one of the quickest and easiest ways for us to get to know each other.

As a way to thank everyone who responds, we'll be sending out a free Adventure Comics poster (featuring the artwork from the cover of *BAD AXE #1*) plus a special surprise from our back room. So send in the completed form today, before all the good surprises are gone.

Name_____ Age _____

Address_____ Sex:___Male___Female

City/State/Zip_____

Marital Status:____Single____Married ____Divorce

Education: Indicate highest level reached

____ High School Graduate ____Two-years college

____Four-years of college ____Graduate School

Comic this form was taken from

_____

Dollars spent on comics per month - $_____

**Dollars spent on paperbacks
and other magazines per month- $ _____**

Do you own real estate ____Yes ____ No

**Hours of television
you watch per week _____hours**

**Numbers of visits to
movie theatres per month _____visits**

Yearly gross income:

____$0 - $10,000   ____$10,000 - $15,000

____$15,000 - $20,000   ____$20,000 - $30,000

____$30,000 - $40,000   ____$40,000 - $50,000

____$50,000 - $60,000   ____more than $60,000

Comic book companies you regularly buy from:

____Aardvark-Vanaheim____Adventure ____Aircel

____Apple ____Archie ____Blackthorne

____Caliber Press____Comico____Continuity

____Dark Horse ____DC ____Eclipse ____Eternity

____Fantagraphics ____First ____Gladstone

____Kitchen Sink ____Last Gasp____Marvel

____Mirage ____New Comics ____NOW

____Piranha____Rip Off ____Slave Labor ____Viz

____Other_____

Comic fan magazines you regularly read:

____ Amazing Heroes ____Comic Buyer's Guide

____Comics Journal   ____Comics Interview

____Comics Scene   ____Speakeasy

____Starlog   ____Fangoria

Return this form to:
Malibu Reader Survey
1355 Lawrence Dr. #212
Newbury Park, CA 91320

Name and address is optional - but necessary for free gift!